This

Angelina

book belongs to

. . . .

PUFFIN BOOKS

Published by the Penguin Group:
London, New York, Australia, Canada, India, Ireland, New Zealand and South Africa
Penguin Books Ltd, Registered Offices: 80 Strand, London WC2R 0RL, England

puffinbooks.com

Angelina on Stage first published by Aurum Press Ltd 1986; published in Puffin Books 2001
Angelina and Alice first published by Aurum Press Ltd 1987; published in Puffin Books 2001
This collection first published 2011
002 – 10 9 8 7 6 5 4 3 2

ISBN: 978–0–141–33529–2

Angelina's Showtime Collection

Story by *Katharine Holabird* Illustrations by *Helen Craig*

PUFFIN

Angelina
and Alice

Story by *Katharine Holabird* Illustrations by *Helen Craig*

Angelina jumped for joy the day Alice came to school.
Alice loved to dance and do gymnastics, and was
good at all the same things as Angelina. They quickly
became close friends and were always together. At breaks
they skipped rope and did cartwheels round and round
the playground.

They loved to see who could
hang upside down longest
on the trapeze bar without
wiggling, swing highest on
the swings, or do the most
somersaults in the air.

Angelina was good at cartwheels and could
even do the splits, but Alice could do
a perfect handstand with her toes
pointed straight in the air, and
never lose her balance.

Angelina always fell over when she tried to do a handstand, which was embarrassing, especially on the playground.

One day Angelina fell right on her bottom and the older
children pointed at her and laughed. One of them giggled
and said, "Look at Angelina Tumbelina!" Another
whispered to Alice, and then …

… something awful happened. Alice giggled too, and ran off to play with the older children while Angelina sat behind the swings and cried.

The next day was worse. They were all saying, "Angelina Tumbelina!" in the playground, and Angelina couldn't find Alice anywhere. Angelina couldn't concentrate at school and made lots of mistakes in her spelling. She couldn't eat her sandwiches at lunch either, and by the time the class was lining up for sports, Angelina felt so sick she wished she could go home.

Mr Hopper, the sports teacher, blew his whistle for silence and said, "You've all worked so hard at your gymnastics over the year that we are going to do a show for the village festival. Everyone needs to find a partner and start practising now."

Angelina looked at the floor. Who could she ask? She was afraid nobody would be her partner. A big tear rolled down her nose.

Then she felt a tap on her shoulder. It was Alice!
"Will you be my partner, please?" Alice asked.

All that afternoon Angelina and
Alice worked on handstands in the
gymnasium. "Just keep your head
down and line up your tail with the
tip of your nose," Alice said patiently.
"That always helps me to stay up
straight longer." Alice was a good
teacher, and soon Angelina could do
a handstand without falling at all.

Mr Hopper taught them how to swing in a beautiful circle over the bar, and how to actually fly through the air and land neatly balanced on the mat.

He taught them to work with the rings and on the bars

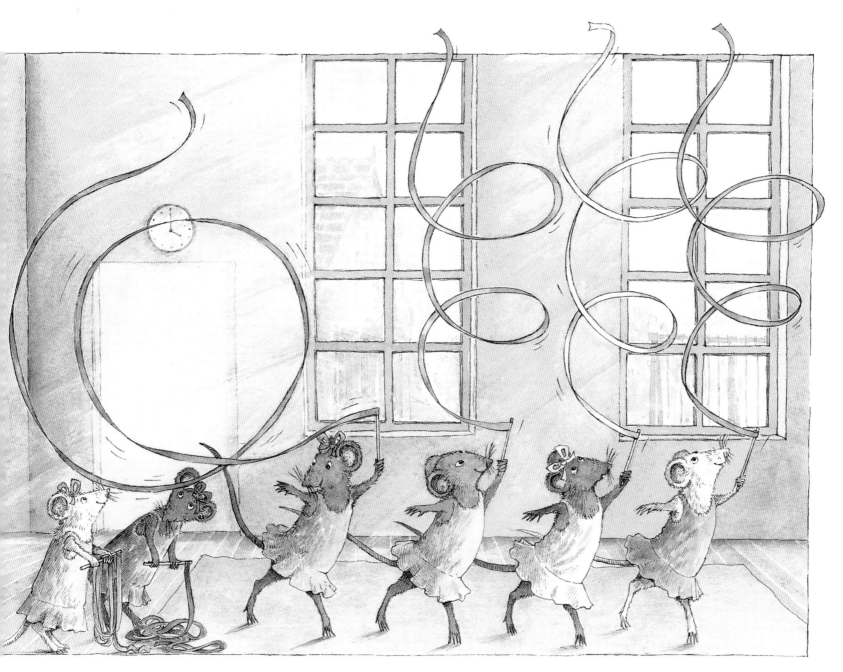

and to do rhythmic gymnastics with coloured ribbons.

Finally, Mr Hopper showed them a
terrific balancing trick they could
do for the show.

The day of the village festival was
bright and beautiful.

The gymnastics class did a wonderful display at the village festival with high jumps, back flips, and balancing on the bars. When Angelina and Alice did their balancing act together even the older children were impressed. "Wow!" they said. "How did you learn to do those amazing tricks?"

PIN THE TAIL ON THE CAT & WIN A PRIZE!

After the show, Mr Hopper smiled and
said, "That was really good teamwork!"
Alice and Angelina grinned back.
"That's because we're such good
friends," they said together.

Angelina on Stage

Story by Katharine Holabird Illustrations by Helen Craig

Angelina's cousin Henry liked to go to her ballet lessons at Miss Lilly's and join in the dancing. Henry always followed close behind Angelina, copying her graceful steps, but he wiggled and wobbled and didn't look like a ballet dancer at all.

After each class, Angelina showed Henry the *right* way
to do the pliés and arabesques and twirls.

But Henry kept on dancing in his own funny way.

Then one day Miss Lilly received a letter from Mr Popoff,
the great musical director. "Angelina," said her ballet teacher,
"how would you like to be a magic fairy in a real grown-ups'
ballet?" Angelina was thrilled. "Oh, yes!" she cried.

"It is called *The Gypsy Queen*," said Miss Lilly excitedly. Then she turned to Henry. "Mr Popoff needs a little elf too, and you are the perfect size."

"Hooray!" shouted Henry, but Angelina just crossed her fingers for good luck, hoping he wouldn't do anything too silly.

At rehearsals Angelina learned to fly through the air with a special wire attached to her costume so that she looked like a fairy floating down out of the sky. Henry was supposed to scamper through the woods below looking for the fairy, but he often got mixed up and went the wrong way.

All the actors and actresses adored Henry anyway, and during the breaks, the lovely Madame Zizi gave him little treats in her dressing room. Then Mr Popoff decided that Henry should say something on stage, and Angelina felt very jealous.

Everyone cheered when Henry came on stage and said in his little squeaky voice, "There goes my friend, the magic fairy!" But he was not so good at finding his way from the dressing room to the stage and was always getting lost.

On the night of the first
performance, everyone
backstage was very excited.
Angelina waited in the wings
with her crown on and her
wand ready as the audience
crowded into the theatre and
the orchestra began to play.
Madame Zizi glanced around
nervously and said, "Oh dear,
where's my little elf?"

Angelina ran wildly through the corridors looking for Henry ...

… and bumped into him as he was running the wrong way down the hall. "I got lost again!" Henry sobbed as Angelina grabbed his hand and raced back to the stage.

Angelina had her special wire fastened just in time.
She soared up over the trees waving her magic
wand as Henry jumped out from the wings
and skipped through the woods to the
front of the stage.

Henry turned and saw the theatre filled with lights and a sea of strange faces. He couldn't open his mouth. He just stared out at the audience.

For an awful moment nothing happened.

"Serves him right," thought Angelina, still feeling annoyed, but when she looked down and saw how terrified Henry looked, she felt sorry for him.

Angelina waved her magic wand and called to Henry in a loud, clear voice, "Hello, little elf, can you see me?"

Henry looked up with relief and said, "There goes my *best* friend, the magic fairy."

At the end of the show, Angelina and Henry took
a curtain call with all the actors and dancers.

The audience cheered and clapped, and the director
thanked everyone for a wonderful performance.

Madame Zizi gave Angelina some of her own roses, and Mr Popoff smiled at her and said, "You're a fine actress, and you'll have a speaking part too, from now on."

Angelina was so pleased that she took Henry by the hands and waltzed around the stage with him until they were both very dizzy.